Taming Wells

Book 3.5 of the FORBIDDEN series
A Jasper Wells novella

Z. S. STORM

Copyright

Blurb

*Join Jasper on his journey during the first few years post moving to Pavia.

Playlist

*Imagine Dragons: Whatever It Takes
   *Nelly : Just A Dream
   *Linkin Park : Numb
   *Maroon 5 : Payphone
   *Jojo : Say Love
   *Mabel : Boyfriend
   *Chvrches : Miracle

****

Full playlist can be found on my YouTube channel:
   Z. S. STORM[1]

---

1.   https://www.youtube.com/playlist?list=PLLCoTPhpN2_mYPzqQYSQwoZCs0Cvn05ue

Dedication

To every Jasper Wells fan

Chapter 1

<u>**Jasper**</u>

"I think I'm going to enjoy living here," I declared loudly as I stood in the middle of the living room of our new home in Pavia. The place was huge. I'm talking five bedrooms, a pool and a game room kind of huge with two home offices. Perfect for our family.

"I'll bet," Skye's muttered voice came from behind me.

I frowned a little at her tone. Please God no. Not the Jasmine thing again. That had been her main concern when we had been deciding which place to buy around here but Armaan had been able to persuade her and Cole to move in next door. The architect in Cole had seen the beauty in the design and structure of this place and the artist in Skye, after falling in love with the scenic views, hadn't been able to resist in the end.

I turned to find her rocking her son to sleep as she paced around the living room. Cole was upstairs taking a shower or something. I was overdue for one as well. Tonight was my night with him. My lips curved as I thought about it but then I blinked at Skye, seeing that she was having a little trouble with the baby who began crying continuously.

Benjamin. They'd named him Benjamin Aimeric Sawyer. My son had a brother now.

"Give him to me," I said to her, striding over to take the boy. "You're exhausted. Let me look after him for a while."

She gave me a grateful look and handed Ben over to me. Jacob was already in bed since it was almost nine.

"Do you need Cole to stay with you, tonight?" I asked her gently. She looked tired and so tense. The baby had been giving her a hard time since this afternoon.

Skye shook her head at me. "That's okay," she replied softly. "I'll just take a nice, long bath and read or something. Today was so hectic." Her expression was regretful as she smoothed a hand over Ben's head. "It just gets exhausting. I don't know why-"

"It's fine, Madison," I said and jerked my chin upstairs. "Go get some downtime."

Ben was quiet now which caused her to appear really confused. Cole had told me she'd faced the same problem with Jacob. Post-natal depression or something. She'd cheered up when he'd proposed to her though.

A laugh escaped me and it made Skye pause on her way upstairs to regard me suspiciously. "What's so funny?" she asked.

I gave a shrug. "Nothing. I was just wondering if a proposal would cheer you up again."

Her blue eyes narrowed at me. "You'd be the last man on earth I'd marry," she declared confidently.

I cocked my head at her. "I wasn't talking about myself," I murmured. "I meant maybe from Cole. You guys could renew your wedding vows. Have a bigger, happier function this time around."

Skye let out a sigh. "Jasper," she said in a low voice. "You don't have to do that." She paused, her hands resting on the banister. "You don't have to keep making me feel like I belong. I'm happy you and Cole are together. It really doesn't bother me. I know he'll always love me."

I studied her for a while and nodded. "As long as you're happy," I replied with a smile.

I always worried about her. It had been a year but that didn't mean we started to take things for granted. Skye deserved so much love and happiness. She belonged right here with us. I knew Cole would never hurt her but...it still didn't stop me from reassuring her every now and then that my relationship with Cole didn't in any way undermine what she had with him.

"Good night, Jasper," she said and retreated upstairs.

I looked down at the baby, sleeping soundly now in my arms. I didn't understand why kids loved me so much when I had no experience with them and wasn't exactly sentimental or adoring. Walking over to the nursery, I gently lowered Ben in his cot. Family. I had a family now. It overwhelmed me so much sometimes, to know that after all the wrong things I did, I ended up finding my happy place anyway.

My sister, Catherine, came inside the nursery just as I straightened and gave me a bright smile. "Hey, bro. I'm going to go next door for a bit, okay. Sophia invited me to look at some of her designs."

I frowned at her. She'd only met Armaan's brother's girlfriend this morning. I knew she was twenty three and an adult now but I still felt protective of her.

"It's almost nine," I pointed out.

Catherine gave me a shrug. "Well, Armaan's having a late night party. Apparently, he does that a lot. You guys are super boring right now. Let me live a little."

I didn't like it. I wasn't sure why but I just didn't like it. Her getting along with Armaan and his friends after having only met them. She was my sister. I know I wasn't supposed to notice such things about her but I did. The way she had been looking at Armaan...

"Don't stay out too late," I told her gruffly. "Keys are on the kitchen counter."

She gave me a thumbs-up and left. My parents were asleep too after the exhausting day so I decided to turn in since there wasn't much else to do. It kind of bugged me a little. Super boring? Was that what we were? I had never heard myself being described that way before. It didn't sit well with me.

When I entered my room, I found Cole standing by the bed, flipping through a book, dressed in his sleep shorts and looking smoking hot. I so wanted to hit that right now but...

"I think you should spend the night with Skye."

He gave me a look over his shoulder. "Why? What happened?" he asked, putting the book down and walking over to me slowly.

I shrugged. "She seems...a bit down. Just go be with her."

He frowned at me a little before leaning in to give me a kiss. "Are you sure?" he whispered.

I nodded. "Yeah." We kissed again and then he pulled back to give me a concerned look.

"Are you okay?" he asked me.

I *had* been until the conversation downstairs.

"You don't think I'm boring now, do you?" I asked him abruptly.

Cole raised his eyebrows at me. "Whoa. Where's this coming from?" He laughed shortly.

I shrugged before brushing past him to head over to the ensuite bathroom. "I don't know. Jasmine called me tame. Catherine called me super boring. I mean, do *you* think that about me too?"

I heard him sigh. "Wells," he began in his serious voice. "I really don't think that. At all. But...just so you know, boring is not a bad thing." He paused and then added, "However, if you're getting restless, just let me know what's on your mind. We'll work something out."

Turning, I gave him a puzzled look. "Huh?"

Cole smirked at me. "I mean, if you want to be...a little adventurous, maybe?"

What the hell was he going on about? Adventurous how?

He didn't elaborate though; just gave me a wink and mouthed 'good night' before leaving.

After I had showered and lay down in my bed with a movie playing on my phone, I thought about his words, his meaning dawning upon me slowly.

No. There was no way he was serious. He *couldn't* be serious.

Right?

****

Chapter 2

"I didn't think you were serious," I said to my boyfriend as we sat in one corner of a bar nearby our place in Pavia.

Cole and I hadn't been to a bar in years so when he had brought me here for a date tonight a week after we had moved here, I'd been mildly surprised. My parents had returned to London but Catherine had stayed back, deciding to extend her vacation for another two weeks. She was at home with Skye and the kids tonight. Cole insisted we needed a boys' night-out but an hour after arriving, he was chatting up a girl.

For me.

She had just excused herself to go to the bathroom.

"I think you need it," he said to me, fixing his green gaze on me, light reflecting off his glasses. "When you tell yourself you don't, you end up doing way more damage so just relax."

I felt uneasy. He was trying to fix me up with a woman because he thought I needed it. That if he didn't let me do it, I'd just go behind his back and cheat again.

"You really don't trust me, do you?" I muttered, looking down at my glass of chilled water.

"It's not about that," he replied, reaching out to place a hand on my arm. "I know it wouldn't mean anything to you. You love me."

God, I was a sick bastard. And Cole Sawyer, the man who knew me better than anyone, could probably tell. No matter how hard I tried to rein in my wildness, as soon as I got over my grumpy moods, I felt the need to just go and do something reckless. It had started after I recovered from my first stroke. Periods of inactivity and depression followed by acts of indulgence that a man like me who was in a committed relationship had no business indulging in.

"Let's go home, Sawyer," I sighed, making an attempt to dissuade him from what he thought I needed. Something I didn't really want to dwell upon.

I'd made my peace with life. I'd come home and was glad to be with my family. The family I had almost lost for good if it hadn't been for my best friend's interference. I should be content with that.

"So, where were we?" The girl, whose name escaped me, slid into the booth next to me and gave me a wink.

I regarded Cole with a blank expression. My absolutely patient and completely understanding partner just grinned at me, stood up, patted my back and then left me the car keys before announcing he was going to take a walk.

He'll take a walk, all right. All the way home.

I dropped my face in my hands after he left me with the chick. I felt her hand pressing into my arm a minute later.

"God, I love your muscles," she breathed out in an awed voice, her thigh rubbing against mine underneath the table.

I was going to hell.

<p style="text-align:center">~~~</p>

I woke up the next morning to find the girl in bed next to me. I almost blacked out from shock. Nothing. I had no memory of last night whatsoever after Cole had left me with her.

What the fuck?

"Hey." I prodded her shoulder, even more confused to find myself naked. Had we had sex? Why didn't I remember anything? All I'd had to drink was water. "Hey, you need to get out of here," I said a bit loudly and shook her a little. She barely stirred.

Cole. I needed to find Cole. I was starting to panic here.

Wrapping the sheet around my hips, I walked over to the door and opened it to find my boyfriend already approaching my room. My mouth was so dry and brain foggy as fuck. I *knew* I hadn't had any alcohol so why did it feel like I was hungover?

"Cole, I have to talk to you."

He looked so smart and attractive in his suit, the clean smell of him reaching me right before he did. Before I could explain, he frowned over my shoulder and said, "Jesus, Wells. You didn't have to bring her home."

I started to shake my head at him.

"Listen, I'm getting late for work so see you tonight?" He leaned in to kiss my mouth, seemed to think better of it and just smiled at me. "Please take a shower," he told me smoothly. "And get rid of her."

He frowned at his watch then and walked away as though seeing a woman in my bed was something that happened every day. I just stared at his back as he hurried downstairs before shaking my head to clear it and going back into the bedroom to wake the girl up again. This was a very, very strange situation...even for me. How did she even know where I lived?

I needed something other than water to drink. Maybe some fruit juice to get my brain functioning again. After taking a quick shower and pulling on some pants, I growled at the girl to get up because I was starting to lose my patience. When I opened the door to go downstairs, I came face to face with Skye.

"Skye," I said a little too loudly and quickly while pulling the door close behind me.

She was holding a basket of my laundry which I took from her immediately. "You didn't have to bring it up. I would've gotten it myself."

She gave me a small smile and opened her mouth to reply.

"Hey, do you have any coffee around here?"

The expression on Skye Madison's face probably mirrored mine at that moment.

Absolute horror.

She made as if to open my door but I blocked her. Skye shot me a murderous look before pushing me aside and walking inside my room. Her mouth fell open in shock when she saw the girl in my bed, who was now conveniently awake and blinking up at us.

"Skye, it's not what you think-"

She whirled around and pinned me with a glare. "I don't believe this," she hissed at me. "What is *wrong* with you, Jasper?"

"Look, I don't know how-"

She scoffed at me. "I should've known it wouldn't last," she muttered, walking out while shaking her head. "The I'm-a-changed-man act. How could you do this? There are *children* living here. Oh my God. How would Cole feel?!" she shrieked at me suddenly and I winced.

"Skye, listen to me. Last night-"

"You." She stopped me with a finger pointed at me. "You...are the most *disgusting* man on this earth."

I shut my mouth then. I just stood there and took it. Nothing I said would get through to her, anyway.

"God." She threw up her hands and paced a little. "This mess. You keep creating this mess in our family just when everything starts to go well." Her blue eyes spat fire at me. "You and your dick need some serious therapy!" she finally yelled before stalking off.

****

Chapter 3

"Oh my god...she actually raped you."

Jasmine was holding her stomach and laughing after I told her what happened this morning. The girl had a very strange personality. One minute, she'd be cold and uncaring with her remarks and the next, you'd find her giggling like a schoolgirl at the weirdest things.

"It's not funny," I muttered, kicking around the soccer ball I'd found lying in the field behind their house.

Apparently, her lover sponsored some local soccer team and they practised here regularly. Sometimes, Jasmine even joined in.

"It's a little funny," she giggled as she looked at me with watery eyes. "I can't believe a big, tough guy like you fell for that trick. Also, I've lived in Pavia longer than you, Jasper." She took the ball from me and rolled it back and forth between her hands. "The girls here are very interested in the hot new piece of ass in town. They don't see a ring on your finger so they've probably been fighting over who gets first dibs."

That was news to me.

She was quiet for a while as she looked at my disturbed expression before starting to snicker again.

"You have such a twisted mind," I told her.

Jasmine held up her hands. "Dude. When have I ever denied that?"

I just shook my head at her before frowning into the distance. "Should I press charges or something? I'm feeling kind of violated."

She clamped her lips together but her eyes glinted with repressed glee.

"Never mind," I grumbled and then turned my attention to Jacob who had finally returned with the ball I had kicked to the far corner of the field a minute ago.

He placed it on the ground before attempting to kick it himself and when he managed to get it right, a huge grin formed on his face.

"I think he's going to grow up to be a soccer player," Jasmine said in a matter-of-fact tone. "Armaan was telling me he could sense these things in kids. If they have that soccer drive in them or something. Like they're naturals with the ball."

I let out a grunt. He could be a soccer player if he wanted. I had no problems with that. I only wanted Jacob to be safe and happy no matter where he was and what he did in life.

"Why does he keep doing that?" she asked me suddenly and I followed her gaze to find my son staring at her. Again.

I smirked a little. "Maybe he thinks you're twisted too."

She rolled her eyes at me. "I have to go write now. I'm almost done with my latest book."

I gave her a nod and was about to say goodbye when I heard my sister up in the balcony of their double-storey mansion, laughing at something Armaan said. His brother Alex and the girlfriend were there too but Catherine only had eyes for Armaan.

My eyes met Jasmine's in a worried look. "Doesn't that bother you? I've told her not to come here that often but she's not listening to me."

Jasmine just shrugged. "Relax, Wells. She's just having a little fun. He won't do anything."

I stared at her. "How do you know that?" I asked because I was genuinely curious. This girl didn't even trust her own shadow much less any other person.

Her response was to present me with a wicked smile. "I *know* because I've got him wrapped around my finger," she told me with a twirl of her index finger. "Besides, sometimes it turns me on to know somebody's lusting after him. Makes me want to ravish him even more. Makes the sex hotter," she whispered that last part so that Jacob wouldn't hear.

My best friend, ladies and gentlemen.

"Like I said," I murmured, taking my son by the shoulders and walking off. "Twisted."

****

Chapter 4

Dinner that night was awkward as fuck. It was just the three of us. Catherine was in the game room watching a movie with Jacob who had eaten early and Ben was asleep so that left Skye, Cole and I at the table.

One year. We had had peace and joy for one year. So much that we had made others envious when they saw the harmony and love we represented as a blended family. And it only took one misunderstanding from this morning to rip that motherfucking peace into shreds of darkness weighed down by past resentments.

I got it. I really did. It's not like I hadn't expected this. That cheating stamp would forever be on my face and even if Skye and I had broken up, she would find any reminders of my infidelity triggering. So I understood her outburst. It was one of the reasons I had been so reluctant to make amends with her years ago. Some people could forgive but they couldn't forget. How could I even blame her after everything I'd put her through? But if only she would listen to me....

Cole got a call from a client so he went in his office to talk. I decided to help Skye out with the dishes to appease her distraught state of mind somewhat. She was still looking at me like I was scum.

"Go upstairs and rest. I'll take care of this," I said to her quietly because she looked tired again.

The gallery in Milan was doing well but Skye's director, Leo, was now mostly in charge of its running whereas she went in a few times a week to check in and conduct lessons or see to meetings with any new artists. It couldn't be easy juggling all that while suffering from post-natal depression. It was a good thing she had Cole to take care of her.

Ignoring my attempts to help, Skye continued to stack up plates in the dishwasher. Suddenly, I started to feel pissed off. Not only did she not want to hear an explanation but she was also determined to act as though I had done her some great wrong. This was my parents all over again. The same silent treatment, the outbursts, the lack of trust and insane amounts of suspicion. No meaningful communication whatsoever. Well, she wasn't the only one who could be triggered by reminders of the past. I didn't know how my father had borne it all for so long without giving up because fuck, I wanted to break something out of pure frustration at that moment.

I eyed the plate in my hand. Skye snatched it from me and started the dishwasher.

"You know, even if I did sleep with that girl out of my own free will which I didn't, I don't get what your problem is," I growled, unable to hold it in any longer. "That's between me and Cole."

She rolled her eyes. "Sure it is. And my poor husband who just can't bring himself to say no to you will give in to whatever you need every time. A trait of his you take advantage of a little too often."

I gritted my teeth. "He's my boyfriend too, Skye. I wouldn't ever hurt him like that again. And did you even hear what I said-?"

She held up her hand, giving me a long-suffering look. "It's not going to work on me," she said gravely just as Cole appeared behind her. "Whatever tricks you resort to to get your precious Cole to agree to all your demands, I can see right through them all."

I widened my eyes at her while Cole just stood there and stared.

"Madison-"

"No, Jasper," she snapped. "I'm just glad I came to my senses and realised exactly what a huge mistake you were. I can't expect Cole to do the same because he's obviously too blinded by his love for you even if you hurt him-"

"Shut up," I bit out, glaring at her.

Skye stopped speaking to look at me warily. I glanced back at Cole who seemed rooted to the spot, his face pale. Finally, Skye followed my gaze and her jaw went a bit slack upon seeing her husband there.

"Cole," she whispered, turning towards him. "Baby-"

"I need some air," he mumbled before turning around and exiting the kitchen.

~~~

He came to me late at night, just crawling into bed and pressing his bare chest to my back. We didn't speak for a long time.

"I trust you, Wells," he breathed into my neck and for some reason, it made my eyes tear up. "Please don't mind her words. She's...just going through a lot," he added.

I clenched my jaw at the pain I detected in his tone despite his attempts to sound normal and brought up a hand to cover his which was draped over my chest.

"I didn't pick up that girl, Cole. She drugged me. I tried to explain it to Skye."

He lifted his head then. "Wait, she drugged you?" he rasped out in surprise. "Shit. Wells, that's...that isn't right. Do you want to report it?"

I closed my eyes at the concern in his tone. For the first time since last night, I found myself smiling. Precious Cole, Skye had called him. Damn right he was.

"I love you," I murmured and shifted to face him. "It's okay. I'm okay." His hands rubbed my chest absently and I felt myself grow hard at his touch and nearness.

Our lips met and I gave him lingering kisses which grew more heated as the force of love and desire pushed down upon us in that darkened room. I was nibbling on his neck when he spoke into the silence and his words made me go still.

"I think Skye's pregnant again.

****
~~~

Chapter 5

I was shaving in the bathroom the next morning when Cole walked in fully dressed and almost ready to head out. Taking the shaver from me, he turned me around and calmly got to work while I leaned against the sink regarding him with amusement.

"You know, maybe I should go somewhere for a few weeks," I mumbled. "Take Jacob for a vacation."

He paused, his brows coming together in a frown. "No."

I swallowed a little. "I don't want to make things worse for her. Maybe if I give her some space-"

"If you want to go, go for the right reasons, Wells," he muttered, resuming the shaving. "Not because you feel like you're not wanted."

I remained silent then as he finished up the task and rinsed the shaver.

"Would you have forgiven me if I'd had an affair with a guy?" I asked him after a moment.

Cole glanced up at me with a solemn look and said, "Yes."

He didn't elaborate but there was not a single grain of doubt or hesitation in his tone. My heart grew heavy as we stood there gazing at each other.

"I'd have forgiven you too, you know...if you'd...well, if you had ever betrayed me," I choked out.

His expression was so calm, so full of wisdom as he spoke. "You already did."

There was a significant pause. I couldn't even bring myself to speak for a few seconds. Inhaling deeply, I brought my hand up and touched his shoulder.

"Do you remember what you said to me the night we...first had sex?" I asked him in a low murmur.

He appeared puzzled. "I said a lot of things, baby," he replied slowly.

I shook my head. "You told me...that I knew all the right things to say," I reminded him, the memory so vivid because it had been our first time. I smiled at him. "Well now you know all the right things to say, don't you?"

Cole grinned at me wickedly and I growled and pulled him closer. "Come here."

"Wells," he laughed a little and pulled away, wiping his nose. I'd smeared some shaving foam on it.

****

Chapter 6

I was spending a lot of time at Jasmine's place. It had been two weeks since Cole had told me Skye was pregnant and I kept feeling like I was walking on eggshells in my own house. I'd gone to London and then down to the Amalfi coast for work purposes but every other spare moment I got here in Pavia, I came and hung out with Jasmine, bringing Jacob with me. Cole didn't mind. He was busy with work and he was doing his best to be there for Skye so I gave them space.

It was a Friday night and I was in the living room with Jasmine watching Jacob play when Armaan's car pulled into the driveway. He'd gone to Amira for a week because his elder brother and his wife had met with a car accident and there were funeral rites and rituals to be performed. Alex had gone with him whereas Jasmine's friend Sophia had returned to her home.

"I should probably go," I said, starting to get up. "Leave you guys to catch up."

She shook her head at me frantically. "No, no, no. Please don't leave me alone with him right now. He might cry and I don't know how to handle people when they cry."

I gave her an amused look. "You handled me just fine whenever I used to cry," I reminded her.

Her expression turned kind as she remembered. "We're two of a kind, Jasper. When you cried, it felt like I was watching myself cry. And I've been handling myself crying for years," she told me.

I didn't get a chance to reply before her lover walked in. He wasn't alone. There was a kid with him. Jasmine just stared at them, her mouth falling open in surprise.

"Aaru-"

"I'm adopting him," Armaan stated without preamble.

There was silence all around except for Jacob playing with his Batman toys. The kid, who was a boy probably a little older than my own son, flicked a hesitant but curious glance at Jacob.

"I know if I'd asked you, you would've said no," Armaan continued staidly. "Ammi said they would look after him but she's got too much on her plate right now with nobody being there to help Abbu with the business. You don't have to do anything. I'm taking full responsibility for Ziad."

She didn't say anything as he led the little boy away towards the stairs, her expression looking sort of haunted. I stayed silent as well because I didn't know how to respond at first to such a bizarre situation. What do you do when the man you're in a live-in relationship with suddenly brings his dead brother's child home and announces he will adopt him without even discussing it with you?

"Dad, can you fix this?" Jacob asked me suddenly, bringing me one of his Batman toy cars.

I took it from him absently and then stilled, giving him a surprised look.

"Jacob...did you just call me 'dad'?" I asked with a tiny grin. "Who taught you that?"

Jacob just watched my hands, waiting for me to fix his toy and I lifted his chin gently and repeated my question. He frowned slightly as though it was no big deal, which it probably wasn't for him but for me...I don't know...it felt good. Really good.

"Mummy. Mummy said you're my dad," he explained seriously and then made an impatient face when he realised I was making no attempt to do as he had asked.

I was smiling the entire time I fixed the toy and handed it back to him. When I glanced up towards the other end of the living room, Jasmine was still sitting there, hugging a pillow to her chest.

"You okay?" I asked her quietly.

She shrugged. "Guess he doesn't know me that well, after all," she murmured before letting out a bitter laugh. "He's just a kid who lost his parents. Has he forgotten I know what that feels like?" She gave me a sad smile. "I wouldn't have said no."

I felt bad for her. Relationships were never easy but when your partner misunderstood you or misjudged you, that shit hurt like a mother. Getting up, I walked over to her and gave her a hug. She looked like she could really use one in that moment.

"I'm sure he didn't mean it like that," I reassured her, rubbing her arm. "Just go talk it over. This is a big deal. That's another human being he's adding to your relationship even if it's a tiny one. It's going to change a lot of things."

Jasmine just blew out a breath. "I think I need a drink," she whispered.

"Jasper."

I looked up at the sound of Skye's voice and blinked when I saw her standing there at the entrance of the living room with an angry expression on her face.

"Skye, what're you doing here?" I asked in concern, getting to my feet.

She pointed to Jacob. "I came to take my son home," she said curtly. "It's way past his bedtime and I tried calling you first but your phone was switched off."

I looked from her to Jacob and then back to her. "You didn't have to do that," I replied. "He's fine. I was just about to leave."

Her lips thinned and she regarded me with narrowed eyes before shifting her gaze to Jasmine. I scowled at her, daring her to say what I knew she was dying to say. But she just shook her head and left, reminding me to get him home fast. Jesus. I really hated this. He was my son too. I knew how to look after him. He could fall asleep in my arms and I'd fucking carry him home in the dead of night if I had to and nobody would be able to touch a hair on his perfect little head.

"Go," Jasmine waved me away, throwing her pillow aside and getting up determinedly. "I need to get drunk or high and then *speak* to Armaan. Thank you." She gave me a mock punch on the shoulder and a grateful smile before striding off.

I envied her. At least she'd be able to drink off some of that tension. And maybe fuck it away.

I doubted Cole was in the mood to have aggressive sex tonight what with his job, looking after Ben and then handling the changes in his marriage exhausting the hell out of him. I hated to ask anyway.

"Hey, Jacob," I called out to my son. "Come on, buddy. Let's go home."

~~~~

I came home to find Cole and Skye fighting. Actual, raised-voices and throwing insults kind of fighting. For a moment, I was so shocked that I could only stand there and gawk at them. Jacob, who actually had fallen asleep on the way home, mumbled something against my shoulder and I made myself move, taking him as far away as possible from the commotion.

I tucked him in my own bed this time, smoothing back his hair and frowning as I overheard my name in the fight going on downstairs. Skye was accusing me of disrupting Jacob's routine and Cole was defending me. This was all about me. I sucked my bottom lip through my teeth, ignoring the pang in my heart and the tears in my eyes as well.

I'd promised I wouldn't make them miserable anymore but here I was doing that very thing. Also...I would never accuse her of it now because she was already so upset and her mental health was precarious but...she kept him from me for two years. And now she was getting mad because I loved to keep him around trying to make up for all that lost time. I would never let anything bad happen to him.

Cole had told me last night that he'd explained the date-rape thing to Skye and she'd just replied that I was probably making it up because
~~~~

nobody would be able to take advantage of a man as strong and smart as me. I'd also overheard her saying that sex for me was like oxygen and it didn't matter where I got it from as long as it helped me breathe.

I let out a sigh and held Jacob's hand for a long time as he slept.

~~~

The next morning, I took Cole aside and informed him that I was going to London for a few weeks. I wanted to take Jacob with me but seeing Skye's situation, it felt like I'd just be adding fuel to fire. My decision made my boyfriend anxious because it felt like history was repeating itself but I assured him that wasn't the case. We were both hot-headed, Skye and I, and Cole was getting dragged in the middle of our disagreements. She wasn't even willing to believe a word I said and I knew I didn't want to waste my time trying to convince her.

We needed space.

I left that morning with a heavy heart, trying not to break down and cry when I hugged my boy and explained that I couldn't take him with me. That he needed to take care of his Mummy while I was away or she would be very sad.

It seemed to appease him somewhat. Cole couldn't say goodbye to me so he locked himself in his office and Skye didn't even look up from her painting when I told her I was going to be away for some time.

****
~~~

Chapter 7

I had so much sex that weekend, I lost count of the number of times I did it. Two different women I'd picked up at a bar where I *had* gotten drunk this time. Fucked them as much as I wanted and in every position until I could barely move a muscle after my marathon was over. But it felt good.

Cole knew all about it. I marvelled at his understanding of my nature. At his confidence in me. He really didn't care where or in whom I put my dick as long as I did it with his consent and came home to him without having lost any part of myself.

I went home to my parents' place after I was done indulging in my vices, feeling deeply satisfied in a purely physical sense. Then I accepted a few assignments for the same company that had hired me way back and catapulted me to global fame as a photographer. I focused on my job for the remainder of my stay there and when I reached home in the evenings and got to see Cole and Jacob on video call, I went to bed with a smile on my face knowing that there were people in this world who loved me and were waiting for me to come home.

Me, the Jasper Wells that I really was, ugly parts and all. I knew what I had to do then once I returned to Pavia. Get my goddamnned self-respect back and grow a fucking backbone.

This, trying to make my family life beautiful and having such a strong weakness for my son, had rendered me speechless or hopeless in a lot of areas where I previously would've set my foot down. Things were going to have to change before whatever good feelings that were left in our home just faded into nothing.

My son was not going to grow up listening to the same shit I had. No fucking way. I could either be selfish and subject him to that by staying under the same roof as Cole and Skye or I could put him first and remove myself from the situation while gearing myself up to settle for sharing custody with his mother. It was the only way this would work now.

She didn't get to tell me what to do.

****

Chapter 8

Cole was at work the day I arrived back in Pavia. Jacob was busy watching cartoons and Ben was asleep. Good. Highly convenient, in fact. This would make my job so much easier.

I headed upstairs and knocked on Skye's door.

"Skye," I called out impatiently. "I need to talk to you." A long minute passed and she didn't answer which made me a little worried because I knew she wouldn't just leave the kids alone like that. "Skye?"

I rattled the doorknob only to find that it wasn't locked at all and entered the room, looking around for her. It was empty. But the bathroom door was open and I could hear soft music tinkling out from there. Baby music.

What the...?

She was in the tub, up to her neck in soap bubbles, reading a book. I just stared at her. When she noticed me, her expression grew enraged and she opened her mouth, most probably to tell me off but I stopped her with a hand. No. Not this time, Skye Madison. This time, you listen to me.

"First of all," I began roughly, "It's nothing I haven't seen before. Second, when have boundaries ever really mattered to you since you walked in on me when I was naked in the shower when you first moved in with us in Milan and then last month, barging into my bedroom and invading my private space?"

Skye's mouth was open as she blinked up at me and not a word came out. Yeah, that's right. That mouth of hers that has been running a little too much lately should be taught a lesson. Too bad Cole wasn't the type to do it. Maybe that's why she felt she could get away with it and act like such a bitch all the time.

"Third," I dragged out angrily, gritting my teeth a little, "You imply that I'm irresponsible but then you leave my sons...my son and Ben downstairs alone while you're up in here soaking and reading a book?!"

She flinched a little at my loud tone but then lifted one dripping wet, slender arm out of the water and pointed somewhere behind me. I turned to look at the pristine white shelves lined up beside the door where a multi-room video baby monitor connected to two cameras was resting. Half the screen showed the game room where Jacob was but the audio was muted. The other half was for the nursery where you could see Ben sleeping soundly in his crib. That was where the baby music was coming out of.

I glanced back at Skye whose eyes were blazing now with repressed anger while the expression on her face remained smug. It pissed me off even more.

"Come downstairs when you're done," I snapped and walked away. "We need to set some ground rules."

~~~~

Jacob was on the kitchen table giggling and squirming as I tickled him. God, I'd missed the little bugger. It had been hell without him but I was still glad I'd taken the time to sort out the mess in my head.

Skye came downstairs looking dressed to kill in a little black dress, full-faced make-up and heels with her hair luxuriously falling in waves around her bare shoulders. Honestly, women were so confusing sometimes. It was good to see her taking care of herself but this was a bit extreme.

"Jacob, I need to talk to Mummy, okay," I told my son affectionately, pinching his nose. "Go watch cartoons. And take this." I retrieved a bag of snacks and toys which I had hidden up till now from under the table and handed it to him. "Game room." I pointed towards it and spoke in a no-nonsense tone so that he would know how serious I was.

My son was only too happy to leave us alone.
~~~~

"Sit down," I said to Skye who was lounging against a counter with a cup of something in her hands. She ignored me.

"Sit your ass down, Madison before I start to use my pissed off voice along with some very colourful language which I'm pretty sure you don't want your sons to hear," I bit out more firmly this time.

I would do it. She knew I would do it. I didn't think hearing curses and the occasional yelling from a parent was enough to scar any child but Skye didn't share my views at all so she dragged out a chair and plunked into it.

Removing the paper from inside the pocket of my jeans, I unfolded it and slapped it down in front of her, along with a pen.

Skye frowned at it and then up at me. "What is this?" she asked suspiciously.

"An agreement," I replied, dragging out a chair for myself as well. "For once, let's have a civilized conversation like the two adults we keep forgetting we are and reach some kind of compromise."

She still appeared confused so I sat back, extended my legs without caring that my feet bumped into hers and folded my arms.

"I'm moving out," I told her calmly, watching as her eyes grew wide at my statement. "Not *out* out unfortunately. I'm planning to build myself a separate apartment right next door with a distinctly separate entrance which you are not allowed to use without my permission."

She sucked in a breath and said, "Jasper, you don't-"

"Wait. How many times have you listened to me exactly since we moved here?" I interrupted, pretending to think about it. "Oh that's right. Zero. So you don't get a say in this. That space will be my own and only my boyfriend, his son and mine will be welcome in it. Got it?"

She narrowed her eyes at me. "I see that you're back to acting like an asshole again after a year of pretending not to be one," she said to me in a sweet voice that didn't match her expression at all.

I spread out my arms. "Happy to be back," I told her just as sweetly and then jerked my chin at the paper. "I'd really like us to be one of those ex-couples who don't need to drag their private matters to family court, Skye. Also, I need to make sure that when I'm spending time with my son, it's *my* time so let's decide on something that's both fair and manageable for us."

She chewed on her bottom lip for a while as she studied the paper outlining the days of the week and hours. I hated to do this. To know that I would now only have a fixed amount of time with Jacob every day. It hurt so bad. If I wanted to tuck him in but it was Skye's turn to look after him, I'd have to distract myself by doing something else. Also Cole...I couldn't just walk out of my room now, find him somewhere in the house and give him a kiss.

Everything was going to change. Because she wouldn't let me be.

"Jasper, I'm sorry. You don't have to do this," she said to me in a pleading tone, fixing her huge eyes on me. "Cole would be heartbroken. Jacob wouldn't understand."

"You didn't leave me with much of a choice," I replied wearily. "I can't live like this," I added through clenched teeth. "You seem to keep forgetting that I'm not your boyfriend anymore and that you need to stop trying to keep me in line." Our eyes remained fixed on each other as I spoke. I wanted to make sure I got through to her this time. "Cole is my partner and he loves me just the way I am so please, please stop expecting things from me which I can't give. You can't tame me, Madison. I refuse to be tamed."

After a minute of searching my face and realising I was dead serious, Skye's shoulders slumped. Then she placed her face in her hands and started to cry.

****

Chapter 9

The hot sun was beating down on me as I lay there on the grass behind my house (nope, scratch that) my soon-to-be *former* house. Closing my eyes, I simply listened to the sounds all around me. Cars somewhere in the distance, birds chirping, wind whistling through the trees and Jacob running around playing. I felt it when the sun went behind a cloud, offering me shade and then the weight of my son's body as he crawled on top of my bare torso and lay there with his cheek pressed to my chest.

"Dad," he said in a child-like voice. "Jasper. Jasper. Dad."

I started to grin and then chuckle as he continued testing those two words like he couldn't decide which sounded better. Hell, even I couldn't decide.

"Second time in my life I realised how much I envy you," came a voice from above me.

Armaan Qureshi. I squinted up at him and then at the kid by his side. So sad and quiet. Alone, despite having a hand to hold.

"I'm not going to ask," I said gruffly since I knew exactly what he was talking about. I'd had his ex-wife's complete attention once and now, I had fatherhood.

He let out a sigh, running a hand through his hair. "I'm a little lost here," he confessed dryly. "I know how to be friends with children. Have no clue how to parent them. This is Ziad, by the way."

The kid swallowed a little, darted a glance at Jacob and I, and then tightened his hold on his guardian's hand. I sat up slowly, trying not to appear intimidating but with a guy my size it was hard to achieve.

"Hello, Ziad," I said in a low voice. "I'm Jasper and this is Jacob. Would you like to play with him?"

The boy shook his head and hid behind his uncle's leg who let out another sigh. "This is hopeless," Armaan muttered.

I frowned thoughtfully. "It's all new to him. Give it time, Qureshi."

His worried eyes went to Jacob. "How long did it take him to adjust when you got back?"

I laughed then. I knew I shouldn't but that damned pride that came with knowing you were a natural as a father and had formed an instant, unbreakable bond with your kid even after two years apart, just wouldn't let me be less of an asshole in that moment.

"Like calls to like," I replied simply after Armaan started to regard me sourly.

A minute passed and then he lowered himself onto the grass a few feet away from me. "Jas told me you're moving out," he said in a casual tone. "What, family life not working out for you?"

Jacob bounced over to his toys and I draped my forearms over my raised knees, focusing on the house I no longer considered mine.

"It's better this way," I answered quietly. "For everyone."

He plucked a blade of grass from the ground and rolled it between his fingers.

"I'm...adopting another kid," he confided in a low but determined tone. "A girl this time. There's a long process but...I think I can get it done within a month or so."

That was very surprising for me to hear but I didn't comment.

"I want kids and she doesn't want to get pregnant or take responsibility for any..." he trailed off and stared into the distance.

I studied his profile as he bit his lip and appeared miserable. Jasmine wouldn't bend on this. If she wanted or didn't want something, you couldn't guilt her into changing her mind. I knew that because we were very much alike in that sense.

"Don't push her," I advised. "You know what happens if you push too hard." I paused and then added, "And I really doubt that her not wanting to have kids means that she'd resent you for adopting. You guys just need to learn how to work around that."

He nodded and then jerked his head up suddenly to look around before his eyes landed on his nephew. I looked as well and found him sitting next to Jacob watching my son put together a Lego house. Jacob frowned in concentration, cocked his head to study the structure and then pointed to a red piece next to Ziad. Ziad looked down at the piece of Lego, glanced back at my son who waited patiently and after a moment's hesitation, picked up the piece before holding it out. Taking it from him with a murmured thanks, Jacob went back to complete his task. But then he paused to give the other kid a serious look and pushed some of his toys towards him before resuming his building.

I found myself smiling. Fuck. That was my kid right there. That display of kindness and acceptance was the most beautiful thing I had witnessed all day.

"I need an architect," I said loudly after a few seconds. "Cole would do it but he's busy with work and this might make him sad. He's already upset that I'm moving out even if he respects my decision." I turned to Armaan who was regarding me with a speculative expression on his face. "It doesn't have to be a big place. Can you help me build it?"

He shrugged. "Sure. I'd even do it for free if you let your son work that magic on my nephew every day. And give me some more parenting advice."

He was being generous. I knew he didn't need the money but still...

"Thank you," was all I said.

People became desperate. They did awful things. But my friend believed in his goodness, Cole and Skye did too. He'd accepted me being a permanent fixture in Jasmine's life quite a while ago. Maybe it was time for me to put the past where it belonged as well and get rid of all the bad feelings that existed between us once and for all.

****

Chapter 10

The next few months were hectic. I was busy with assignments but any spare time I had, I threw my back into constructing the new house and found myself enjoying my new, jam-packed schedule. Armaan helped me out with the planning and designing part of it but also turned into errand boy when the role required it. He didn't mind being told what to do which amused me to no extent because finally, I was starting to understand what Jasmine found so appealing in this guy. He caught me smirking as that thought entered my head once and frowned suspiciously but didn't comment.

Cole and a few local guys I had hired as help joined us in building from time to time. Jacob and his new friend Ziad, whom we mostly referred to as Zi, played at a safe distance away while we worked. There was another addition to their play dates though. A two year old girl called Aaliyah whom Armaan had adopted about four months back. Where Jacob and Zi were serious, moody types, she seemed to steal the show with her cheerful and talkative nature even if what she said at that age hardly made much sense.

Ben was in his crawling stages now which kept Adele, the nanny, busy along with Skye. We'd hired a nanny after seeing how tough it had become for her.

Madison had broken down in front of me that day I had announced my decision to move out. I couldn't *not* get up. I couldn't *not* take her in my arms and comfort her because it hurt to see her like that. She cried all over my shoulder for a good, long while until Ben woke up bawling and hungry.

Skye was too upset and his crying seemed to agitate her even more so I fed him with a bottle and cradled him until he fell asleep again after some cooing, gurgling and drooling. Soon after that, Jacob got hungry and wanted me to play ball with him as well so I told Skye to take a nap and that we would discuss everything later.

Later happened only when Cole finally arrived and I was exhausted from all the caretaking. But we managed to talk that night; Skye most of all. She confessed that she had found the girl-in-my-bed scene triggering after discovering she was pregnant because to her, it had seemed as though I had been cheating all over again. Even if things were over between us, that didn't mean she was over all her former doubts and insecurities and a part of her had naturally grown to be possessive of me since I was living with them and we were all so close.

She apologised, I apologised. We set some rules and drew some lines. Cole was upset I couldn't stay but after plenty of reassurance and a very thorough love-making session, he stopped feeling too anxious about it. Our main priority was Skye's mental health then and also making sure that the kids didn't suffer. The nanny was very experienced and had worked with mums facing depression before. She also had qualifications as a former nurse so she was quite a find especially considering how swiftly Skye had gotten pregnant again.

One thing we hadn't been able to agree on was Jacob's schedule once I started living on my own. That conversation brought out some tears because none of us, not even Cole could make such a decision when it came to our son. How do you even decide when you'll keep him and when you won't?

So we compromised. As long as Jacob was happy and well taken care of, he could stay with whomever he wanted, whenever he wanted. He loved all of us so we left it up to him.

I felt happy about it as I strolled into the kitchen of Skye and Cole's home to grab a bite to eat and Skye found me rummaging inside the fridge when she came downstairs with Ben.

"Adele made doughnuts," she offered lightly, indicating a plate of doughnuts on the kitchen table.

Hmm. I hadn't seen that.

I grabbed it and started to leave the kitchen before she called out, "Jasper, not the whole thing, jeez. Leave some for Cole and me."

Shooting her a grin, I placed the plate back in its original spot and bit into a chocolate one before winking.

"I was just messing with you."

She made a face at me but smiled anyway. I reached for Ben saying, "Here let me take him. He could learn a thing or two watching us men at work."

Skye stepped away with a horrified expression. "Are you crazy? He's just nine months old."

My response was to laugh in a mocking, evil manner.

Skye just shook her head at me before wrinkling her nose. "And your sweat stinks, Jasper...seriously, I'm pregnant here. Stay away from me."

She shrieked when I put my arm around her on purpose then, leaning in to give Ben a kiss.

"You like it," I said to her, causing her to roll her eyes before she shoved me away.

****

Chapter 11

<u>**Skye**</u>

He was being all sweet to me today. Why does he have to do that? Why does he have to remind me of how things used to be?

I lied. I lied to them both.

It's not just because I felt triggered because of what happened in the past.

It's because...

I don't know how to tell them that after all these months, seeing how good he is to us all...his devotion to Jacob and adoration of Ben, his loyalty to Cole and respect for me, his willingness and determination to make this family work...somewhere in the middle of all that...I started to fall for him again.

And it hurt so bad when I found that girl in his room. It hurt so bad when I realised that just because he was nice to me for so long, it doesn't mean that Jasper Wells loves me. It hurt so bad that I did the only thing that helped me in that moment. I lashed out at him.

I said all those mean things to him and even when Cole tried to explain the situation to me, I pretended that I didn't care. I cried because I didn't want him to go but more than that, with the pregnancy and my depression, I didn't want to keep making him miserable with my poisonous words and attitude.

How do I even say it? How do I tell my husband that I'm starting to have feelings for Jasper again?

After everything I went through to survive his betrayal, I need to protect myself.

Because even if he cares for me and comforts me. Even if he thinks I deserve to be treated well and that I belong here...

He won't ever love me the way he loves Cole.

He won't ever say those words to me again.

****

Chapter 12

<u>Jasmine</u>

Armaan was playing soccer with the kids in the field one afternoon as I sat on the grass and watched them during intervals while typing up a chapter on my laptop. It was hard concentrating because of the way he laughed and rolled on the grounds just goofing around with toddlers. My beautiful distraction.

This was mostly me now when he interacted with them, just watching from the sidelines. But I was content with it. I liked seeing him happy.

A lemony fragrance reached my nose after a minute. I looked up and saw Skye Madison standing next to me, her eyes fixed on her son who was amongst the group on the playground. Then she looked back at me with an unsmiling expression.

I put up my hands. "I swear I had nothing to do with it. He followed Armaan and the kids here and Jasper knows about it. He said he'll come get him soon."

She didn't reply as she watched the kids playing happily but just folded her arms and stood there. I went back to my task. I really didn't want to get in the middle of this. Kids, parents, play dates...not my scene.

I felt it so strongly after a while...that Skye wanted to say something. God, I hated that about myself...my inability to just remain oblivious to my surroundings. I could lose myself in my words but would still be so aware of what was going on around me. Most of the time, I ignored that sense. But sometimes...

"You know, I can't concentrate when you're looming over me like that," I said to her. "At least sit down or something. The grass isn't poisonous I assure you."

She didn't move for a while but as I kept typing, she finally lowered herself next to me and extended her legs. It was awkward. Super awkward. Like I could feel that awkwardness just seeping into the air around us and making camp there. I let out a sigh.

"Why am I always the odd one out?" she suddenly asked out loud.

I glanced at her warily. What was she talking about?

She plucked a blade of grass, no not plucked, aggressively pulled it out of the ground and frowned at it.

"Cole loves him. You love him. Jacob and Ben love him. Hell, even Armaan is starting to love him. It's so easy for you people. And he's so easy *on* you people," she muttered, sounding frustrated. "Why can't I be like you guys?"

It took me a few seconds to realise that she was talking about Jasper.

I didn't know what to say to her. I mean, Jasper was Jasper. How could you not love that big brute? Yeah, he could be an arrogant, stubborn prick sometimes but man, I'd seen that man break down and cry in front of me while he was drunk out of his mind, just hurting and missing people he cared about so all the other annoying traits of his didn't even register with me unless I needed to knock some sense into him.

Skye looked absolutely tortured. I couldn't believe she was coming to me for advice and to talk after what had happened the last time. Why would anything I say even matter to her right now?

But her pain was so obvious. She wasn't being mean to me. She wasn't regarding me with suspicion or judgement. It felt as though she was just a girl who felt alone and confused and didn't know whom to turn to. I nibbled on my lip trying to think about it. About what to say.

"It's okay to not be able to feel like others do," I tried after a moment of pondering. "Everyone expects you to just get over your inhibitions and fall in line but if you don't feel it, you don't feel it." I shrugged. "That's who you are as a person and there's no need to feel ashamed about it."

Hell, was I even referring to her? Because while speaking those words, I also kept thinking about Armaan and the kids and how I just couldn't bring myself to want them as much as he does. I knew I didn't want to be anyone's mommy.

"By the way, why are we talking about Jasper?" I suddenly asked her, studying her profile. "Is he giving you trouble?"

She let out a humorless laugh. "This would be *so* much easier if he was," Skye answered in a bitter tone. "Even if we did work things out on a personal level someday...I know that he won't ever change his ways. He's too wild. He doesn't like being cornered or kept in line. Cole is indulging his every whim and my husband is happy with the guy but I don't *ever* see myself doing that." She shook her head adamantly. "I can *never* be okay with casual sex outside of a relationship. Like it's a hard limit for me. Why am I so wrong for believing that?" she cried out.

I was freaking out a little. Was she having a nervous breakdown? I glanced over at Armaan but he was on the far end of the field now with the little ones. He was better with these things. Dealing with people and situations. Me, if I wasn't close to someone, I just froze up.

"You should be talking to Cole and Jasper about all this," I said quietly, trying to sound comforting and hoping I was succeeding.

When Skye turned to me, there were tears in her eyes. "I can't," she whispered helplessly. "Cole is...he's running himself ragged juggling so much. Our marriage, his job, his relationship with Jasper, the kids...and then he's always there trying to make sure I'm okay." She swallowed hard and wiped away her tears. "If I say anything about this, I'll just be adding more stress to our marriage. Besides, I'm supposed to be over Jasper, right? He's moving on and he's clearly over me. What would I even achieve by telling him all this?"

My mind was so fucked right now. Like this was all too much to take in. Emotionally.

I kept staring at Armaan and I'm not sure if it was a sixth sense or some sort of awareness he had of me but he looked my way with a frown, took in the scene and said something to the kids before running over to us. He was there in front of us soon, sweaty and a little breathless but saying all the right things to Skye as she cried softly while he held her as though she was a lost little girl.

Maybe she was one in that moment. I was glad Aaru was there when my presence was pretty much useless. I smiled at him softly and he smiled back while rubbing Skye's shoulder.

"It's okay," he was crooning to her. "It's okay, Skye. Do you want to come inside for a while? Maybe talk about it with me?"

She sniffed and then nodded. My heart went out to her. She just needed someone. Anyone. How did the situation get so worse without any of us around her even realising what the core of the matter was? Jasper had said she was having a tough time but Skye Madison wasn't just having a tough time here...

She was in love with Jasper.

And it was tearing her apart.

****

Chapter 13

Jasper

My boyfriend gave me a massage one night. A full body massage complete with candles and oil. I couldn't stop laughing in the middle of it all. He insisted on doing it because I had been working on the house all day while he had been busy spending time with the kids and Skye since it was his day off. I was exhausted from all that hard labour but he had come to my room and asked me to have sex with him.

Rough sex.

He specifically asked me to treat him roughly and make him do all kinds of dirty, depraved things and damn, I can't resist him when he's being like that so despite my bones screaming from exhaustion, I happily obliged because he seemed to really crave it. Cole was always so patient and good in every aspect of his life, giving so much of himself to others. I hardly saw him practising self-care. To wind down, he either read books or asked me to fuck him instead of just making love.

So the massage was like a thank you to me. It started to feel good after a while. I guessed he was experienced in it from taking care of Skye all the time. I let out a satisfied groan as he kneaded the space between my shoulder blades. Fuck, all that hammering had taken its toll on me. And I didn't just mean the house.

"Boy, you're good at this," I whispered, closing my eyes and smiling as though I was in a drug-induced haze.

He leaned in and nibbled on my ear before pressing his lips to my jaw line. "Not laughing now, are we?" he teased in an indulgent voice.

Turning my head to the side, I captured his lips with mine in a slow kiss. It wasn't sexual. I didn't think I had the energy to be sexual right now.

"I love you, baby," I murmured in a sleepy voice.

He rolled off me and I heard him blowing out the candles and putting all the bottles of oil away before settling in bed next to me.

I forced myself to turn over onto my back and look at him. It didn't seem fair to just fuck, get a massage and then fall off to sleep. He'd go back to work in the morning and tomorrow night, he would be sleeping with Skye.

"How are you doing, really?" I asked him.

Cole had his phone out and had begun reading an ebook, his glasses firmly back on.

"I'm okay," he said, reaching out with a hand and rubbing my arm without taking his eyes off the book.

"How's Skye?"

He smiled slightly. "She's doing much better. I don't know what happened but yesterday she was over at Armaan's place for a long time and when she came back, she seemed to be okay. Like she's trying to be better. She's the one who suggested we go to the city today after so long."

I was glad to hear that. To know that she was trying. I wanted my family to be happy and that included the mother of my child.

"Sometimes I can't help but think that...when you're here holding me at nights...then nobody's holding her," I said to him slowly. "She needs it more."

I never interfered in Cole's relationship with Skye. Because I knew I didn't have to tell him how to be a good husband to her. He already was. But people had relapses all the time just when you thought they were getting better and I hoped Cole wouldn't just let things slide from now on.

His response was to narrow his eyes at me and give me an amused look while he shook his foot casually.

"Well if you're that worried," he began lazily, "You could always just join us in bed. Then I can hold both of you at the same time."

I turned on my side facing away from him. Yeah, this wasn't the first time he had teased me about it. Cole would actually be the happiest guy on earth if the three of us ever did start sharing the same bed again.

I realised it wasn't easy for him to split his time between two people equally. When you were sleeping with one, you missed the other, right? And such was his nature that he never complained about it.

But even if I compromised and did it for his sake and even if Skye agreed to such an arrangement, it would only lead to more problems. More drama. I could give a lot of myself to someone who was important to me. But in return what I wanted from them was to let me be myself and not keep making me feel like I was letting them down. So I didn't reply to Cole's suggestion. He didn't realise it wasn't that easy.

Sharing a bed wasn't the main issue here. Skye would always expect a lot from me because that was the kind of woman she was.

And knowing the kind of man I was, I couldn't promise never to hurt her again.

****

Chapter 14

The house was done in the next couple of weeks. I ended up loving the hell out of it. Just a two-bedroom wooden structure with simple furnishings but incredibly easy on the eyes thanks to Cole and Armaan's designing inputs.

It was my man-cave or Batcave as Cole liked to call it. I even painted it black and grey to go with my personality. First thing I did was break open an expensive bottle of scotch and celebrate with the guys. It had been months since my last drink and this was just such an occasion, even Armaan didn't refuse the toast.

I realised that for the first time in a decade, I was going to have a place all to myself. Live alone.

Maybe I was just used to the idea by now but it started to feel really good. Jacob slept over the first night in the bedroom that was especially for him. A strange sort of pride came over me as I said goodnight to him, left his door ajar and bunked on my living room couch in case he got spooked or something. I was going to share this place with my son. Just like Batman. It made me chuckle as I texted Cole for a while until he fell asleep.

Jasmine came over the next day to give her opinions on the place and seemed to envy the shit out of me because my home was the only kid-free one in the area. I just laughed at her while she helped herself to my coffee.

Funny how I'd been dreading this change for months but when it finally happened, I felt like I was free. Free to just be myself and love my son and Cole for the rest of my life. Even my boyfriend had to smile because he realised we'd been worried for nothing. Life was pretty good.

~~~~
~~~~

Skye gave birth to a baby girl a few months later. I didn't go to the hospital because our nanny was unavailable and I had to stay with the boys. When they came home with the baby who looked exactly like Jacob had looked the day he'd been born, I couldn't stop smiling.

Another beautiful addition to our broken but awesome family.

"We want you to name her," Skye said to me that night and I was taken aback by her words.

She nodded at me with a smile. "Cole named Jacob and I named Ben. We wanted you to do the honours this time."

Well, they should have said something before because I didn't know shit about choosing names.

I thought about it that night and the next morning, I went to them and said, "Annabelle."

Skye and Cole just looked at each other.

I burst out laughing because I knew, I knew they were thinking of the horror movie those two nerds.

Skye gave me a smack on the arm when she realised I was messing with them on purpose and Cole just shook his head.

"Isabelle," I said for real this time and smiled at Skye. "Call her Isabelle Madison. I like it."

They did too. Thank fuck because I probably would have gone with Annabelle if they hadn't objected. Names didn't really matter to me. She was going to be one of my people. That's all I cared about.

The two kids from next door and the three from our family quickly became fast friends over time. Nobody left anyone behind when there were play dates.

I started travelling again for work while Skye juggled her time between motherhood and career. The third time around, she got a handle on it which made Cole and I a couple of happy motherfuckers. It was always great to see your family doing well.

Things had worked out for the best despite our move here having started with so many problems and hurdles.

I slept with a few women every now and then when I travelled but by the time my son started to ask me a lot of questions about what I actually did whenever I went away, I kind of started to lose interest in casual sex.

When Jacob turned five, we threw a huge party in the backyard. Everybody was invited; Jas, Armaan, the kids and some of our friends from work and the neighbourhood. My parents and Catherine came as well. Jacob was so happy, it hurt to look at him.

I think I got a little too drunk that night. And Jasmine gave me some weed because she was smoking it and it had been years for me so I smoked it too just for the hell of it. Then I had to go inside my Batcave, taking the joint with me because my head started spinning.

There was a knock on my door a while later. I stumbled over to it and found Skye outside.

"Oh, hey," I slurred. "What's up?"

She studied my face for a few seconds. "Can I come in?"

I blinked at her. "That's probably not a good idea," I murmured.

She inclined her head and regarded me curiously. "Why?" she asked.

"I've just been smoking in here."

Skye gave me a shrug. "I don't mind a bit of smoke."

I raised my eyebrows at her. This was coming from the girl who once told me she hated the weed community.

"No, I mean...it's not about that," I said slowly. "It's just...I'm high and drunk and I'm afraid I'll do something you're gonna make me regret."

Where the fuck did those words just come out from? That could not have been my mouth because I wouldn't say things like that to Skye. I hadn't said things like that to her in years.

Skye was giving me a thoughtful look.

"Do something *I'm* going to make you regret," she dragged out, nodding to herself. "Good choice of words because you obviously won't be regretting anything *on your own*, huh?"

I just looked at her with my mouth half open. What did she want? Why was she here? What was happening?

Her hands came up to my shirt buttons, smoothing over them.

"You know something, Jasper," she said in a matter-of-fact tone. "It's been three years. Five if you count the time you were away from us. And then that year we were all together when Cole brought me in your lives."

Her lips formed a smile, her lemony scent which I had bought for her when she had been pregnant with Jacob and which she still wore teased my nostrils.

"I'd say I've gotten to know you quite well in six years," she continued softly. "And I think...after seeing all of you, the good, the bad and the ugly, I know exactly what's got my husband so devoted to you."

My heart was beating like a mother. She had no idea what she was saying.

"Skye-"

She pulled my head down and kissed me then and her lips pressing against mine after three fucking years set my body on fire. No. This was wrong. This...couldn't happen. We'd both accepted that years ago.

"There's no taming you, Wells," Skye Madison murmured against my lips and then brought up a thumb to wipe her lipstick from my mouth. "I'm not even going to try anymore."

Her arms went around me, her head rested on my chest.

"Someone once told me not to measure a man's worth by his mistakes," she said softly as though she was about to cry. "I should've listened to her three years ago."

She started to sob then as she held me and I just slid my arms around her without even thinking about it. It all felt like a dream. My throat felt so tight. Closing my eyes, I tightened my hold, breathing in her scent like I'd been starved for a long time.

A thought came into my mind, wild and insistent, something I vaguely remembered saying to my best friend once. I'd forgotten about it afterwards because the idea of it had been impossible at the time.

When we all came together, it felt like we belonged together. Like pieces of a puzzle that was now complete.

****

****

Bonus Scenes

Throwback to that Skye and Armaan convo that helped her see things differently. ☺

....

<u>Skye</u>

He offered me some juice once we were inside his kitchen and settled down opposite me after pushing a box of tissues my way. I sniffed and wiped my nose, having cried a lot of my tears out in the field and while walking inside the house with Armaan.

"One-sided love?" he asked in a murmur. "I've been there. Kind of. Sucks, doesn't it?"

I bit my lip and looked outside at the fountain in front of his home.

"How did you know?" I asked him in a whisper.

Armaan shrugged. "I saw the signs. Been spending a lot of time at your place building Jasper's house." He let out a sigh. "I'm sorry, Skye."

I just clutched my head in my hands. "I can't believe this is happening," I said miserably. "I didn't think I'd ever catch feelings for him again but-"

There was a moment of silence.

"Jasper's a good guy," he told me kindly. "I know you were hurt by his cheating but-"

"I can't ever trust him again," I insisted before he could say anything else. "Even if he ends up falling for me too, there is no way him and I can get into a serious relationship and make it work a second time around. We're just...too different."

He nodded at me. "I get it," he replied thoughtfully. "But...does it have to be that complicated?"

I frowned at him. "What do you mean?"

Armaan pursed his lips, blinked his long lashes and shrugged. "I was deeply in love with Jasmine when she suggested a friends-with-benefits situation a year ago," he calmly informed me. "I didn't expect anything from her. In fact, a part of me kept thinking she would betray me again. Or grow tired of me. But it felt good to be with her and so I didn't really let myself worry about tomorrow."

I sat up straight, inhaling deeply and wondering about his words. He made it sound so easy but I'm sure it hadn't been.

"I don't know if I can do that," I mumbled. "Get involved without expectations. Live in the moment. That isn't me."

Armaan grabbed a bottle of water from the counter and sipped from it.

"I understand, Skye," he said after he finished drinking. "I only meant that if being away from him makes you so miserable, then maybe you can meet the guy halfway." He smiled and gave me a wink. "You don't have to decide now, of course. It's not like he's going anywhere."

Reaching out, he patted my shoulder gently. "Just think about it. If you believe it's worth a shot, then go for it. But also, keep your expectations low and just make the most out of those amazing moments. *Only* if you want him badly enough. Don't let yourself get hurt again, Skye."

He was insane. A no-strings-attached relationship with the man I loved? There was no way I could ever do that.

****

Skye

"Mmm, Jasper, I really don't think this is a good idea," I murmured as I felt his stubbly cheek grazing against my neck. "I'm going to be late for work."

His response was to pull me closer against him under the sheets and growl in that sexy way of his.

It was so, so hard to leave his bed whenever we did find the time to hook up. We were all so damn busy most of the time. The kids, our jobs, Jacob starting pre-school and the everyday running of our household.

Early this morning, I'd come to Jasper's place to ask him if he'd seen Jacob's new pair of sneakers and instead of helping me look for it, he'd just pulled me in bed with him. Okay maybe the sneakers had been an excuse to see him because I hadn't for almost a week since he had been away in Rome for one of his photo shoots.

I heard a noise and started to scramble out of bed, afraid that it was Jacob or maybe even Ben. This was still kind of new and uncertain for me, being intimately involved with Jasper without either of us actually committing to anything. I didn't want to involve the kids in it. How would I even be able to explain any of this to them when they didn't even understand normal adult relations yet?

It was Cole who showed up at the door to Jasper's bedroom and regarded us with an amused look.

"I wondered where my wife had disappeared off to when I woke up and found her side of the bed empty," he said in a cheerful tone and then strode over to the bed.

Okay now I really *was* going to be late. Cole slid between the sheets as though he did not have a care in the world and folded his arms behind his head.

"Aah. This is the life," he said with an expression of pure bliss.

I looked at them both and sighed.

"Look, neither of you have work today so this might all be a joke to you but I need to get dressed and leave, please."

Cole just raised one knee and effectively trapped me from the other side.

"Call in sick. Say something came up," he suggested. My workaholic husband suggested that and I couldn't believe it.

"Yeah. Good idea," Jasper murmured in agreement.

I rolled my eyes. These two men...

"Where are the kids?" I asked anxiously.

"I dropped Jacob off at pre-school and Adele just got here so she's with Izzy and Ben."

"Isabelle," Jasper corrected at once, making Cole and I exchange a long-suffering look.

Just because he had picked Isabelle's name, he felt it was an insult to shorten it to Izzy. As though we were making fun of his choice which was ridiculous because he himself had confessed that he hadn't actually cared all that much about the naming process in the first place.

I tried to sit up but Jasper threw one long leg over me whereas Cole gave me a cute, pleading look. Letting out another huge sigh, I fell back in bed causing Jasper to laugh in a low, sexy manner while my husband smiled affectionately and moved to cuddle with me.

"Ohhh, I fucking love this," he said, sounding so excited and boyish.

"I can't believe you guys are making me do this. I hate you both," I muttered.

Jasper gripped my chin suddenly and crushed my mouth with his in a fierce kiss.

"Stop complaining," he ordered me in a gruff voice. "Me and your husband are going to have a little fun with you now and you're going to let us. Okay?"

I swallowed a little and nodded as his eyes darkened. God, I loved him. And I think he loved me too. I didn't know where this was going. Or if I even wanted it to go somewhere. Last time we had given it a label, it had ended badly.

So this time, he made me no promises and I expected nothing from him. All I knew was that it felt good being with him like this. Being with both of them.

And this way, if things ever did go wrong between us again, which I secretly feared will happen at some point when our views clashed in the future, at least Jacob wouldn't be hurt.

I didn't want my son to grow up seeing his parents together, forming some false hope in his heart that we had an ideal relationship and then be shattered when things didn't work out between his father and I.

Jasper was already busy with his head between my legs and a few seconds later, Cole started to groan next to me as well. I realised with a jolt that I wasn't the only one Jasper Wells was servicing under the sheets.

Multi-tasking at its finest.

I bit back a grin and my husband leaned in to give me a passionate kiss as our desire heightened thanks to our mutual lover's skillful hands and mouth.

We were bad. So, so bad.

But when I stopped thinking about tomorrow and just lived in the moment, I had to admit, it felt really, really good.

****

Cole

Jacob's eyes were wide open as he stared at the TV screen in Jasper's living room at ten p.m on a Saturday night. I walked in to see Jasper standing at the kitchen table, cleaning the lens of one of his cameras while my kid...his kid...okay, *our* kid kept his gaze glued to a gory, grisly and dark Batman movie.

Thank God Skye had gone to bed early after spending the entire day hosting an art exhibition at her gallery in the city. If she had come in here instead of me and seen this...

"Hey," I said, going up to my boyfriend and giving him a thump on the shoulder. "How's it going?"

He mumbled something which I couldn't hear above the sound of the movie and I winced a little before searching for the remote and lowering the volume. Jacob still didn't move or even blink.

"I'm starting to worry about him," I said slowly, casting a glance at Jasper. "I mean, these movies-"

I stopped when Jasper shot me a look. Never, *ever* say anything against his Batman movies or the Batman fandom. The guy would skin you alive. Except he wouldn't do that to me because he loved me.

"It's ten p.m, Jasper, come on," I tried again.

Finally, he sighed, put down his equipment, went over to his son and explained that the movie needed to stop. Jacob made a face but only for a few seconds before he got up to go to the bathroom.

I just blinked at Jasper, marvelling at how he managed to handle Jacob so smoothly. The kid would listen to anything he said.

I cleared my throat. "So maybe after you've tucked him in, you can do the same to me," I said cheekily, flicking my eyebrows at him.

His lips twitched in a smile as he came closer to me. "Oh you want to be tucked in now, is it?" he said in a low, sexy manner. We kissed then and my arms went around him while I leaned back against the table.

"Dad, I finished brushing my teeth," Jacob's voice came from behind him.

Pulling away from me, Jasper gave his son an affectionate smile and scooped him up in his arms.

"I'll be right back," he said to me before taking Jacob into the other room.

I made my way into Jasper's bedroom and toed off my shoes before getting in the huge bed that always looked so sensual and inviting with its black and grey silk sheets and fluffy pillows. Five minutes later, he joined me and we lay there in the dark not speaking for a long while.

"He's a tough kid, you know," Jasper said quietly. "He doesn't get scared easily and if he does, I'm always here."

"Hmm." I smiled a little because I knew Jasper wanted to be the boss of Jacob most of the time but he also understood that I would always worry about the little guy.

"Skye?"

I shifted to face him, the sound of crickets outside his bedroom penetrating the silence.

"She wants to sleep alone tonight. It was an exhausting day," I explained. "You wouldn't have let her rest if I'd asked you to come over."

He chuckled softly at my words and brought out a hand to rub my chest.

"I'm actually tired as well," he murmured. "I did a lot of work today editing and stuff for my latest shoot."

My response was to yawn. I guess we all were tired tonight.

"Good night, baby," I whispered, pressing myself against his warm body.

He put his arm around me just as I closed my eyes.

So many years, twelve, in fact...and yet, I was still so deeply in love with this guy. Every night felt like the first night we had spent together.

It didn't take long for his breathing to even out and I smiled to myself.

Three beautiful kids and two incredible lovers. A family that had survived so much and was still so full of hope and happiness. For a boy who had grown up feeling alone and unloved most of the time with no place he could ever call his own, this was the most beautiful gift life could ever give him.

~~~~
~~~~

'Shameless'

(Book 4 of the FORBIDDEN series Official Teaser)

I was staring at him. I didn't think I had ever stood this close to him before. Especially not since he had grown up into a teenager. He had only just celebrated his eighteenth birthday a few months back and I hadn't even given him a hug. Just a smile and a present that Cole and I had picked for him.

Zi was frowning at me as though he was trying to figure something out. "Mrs. Sawyer," he whispered, his lips curving slightly. "Is everything all right?"

His words made me inhale sharply and step away from him in horror. What was I doing, standing there staring at a teenage boy like that? And so close, I'd felt his breath on my cheek.

"Yes. I'm sorry. I was just...lost in thought," I explained with a nervous laugh.

He nodded again, in his usual polite manner, and turned to walk out of the kitchen. I watched him leave with a hand over my heart, feeling a little uneasy but before he disappeared from my line of sight, he glanced over his shoulder and smiled at me.

It was an innocent smile. Just a friendly one like you would give to your friend's mom or dad when you ran into them.

So why did it feel like he kind of knew the thoughts that had been running through my head in that moment?

****

Other Books by Z. S. STORM

<u>FORBIDDEN series</u>

<u>'Forbidden' (Book 0.5 - prequel. Jasmine's story.)</u>[1]
<u>'Three's A Crowd' (Book 1)</u>[2]
<u>'Once A Cheater' (Book 2)</u>[3]
<u>'Twice Inflamed' (Book 3)</u>[4]
<u>'Taming Wells' (Book 3.5 - A Jasper Wells novella)</u>[5]
<u>'Shameless' (Book 4)</u>[6]
<u>'Wicked' (Book 5)</u>[7]
And many more...

1. https://www.goodreads.com/book/show/55881993-forbidden

2. https://www.goodreads.com/book/show/55716260-three-s-a-crowd

3. https://www.goodreads.com/book/show/55759085-once-a-cheater

4. https://www.goodreads.com/book/show/55759148-twice-inflamed

5. https://www.goodreads.com/book/show/55881985-taming-wells

6. https://www.goodreads.com/book/show/55882058-shameless

7. https://www.goodreads.com/book/show/55882064-wicked

Acknowledgments

Thanks for reading 'Taming Wells'. I wrote it especially for those readers who can never get enough of Jasper.

Shout out to all my loyal and supportive ZStormers. Thanks for your passion for my stories. I'm so glad I started this journey with you all.

I'm so grateful to have a chance to put my books out there. Hope they make a difference in someone's life.

Lots of laughter,

Z.

About the Author

Lover of Batman and forbidden stuff.

***

For future updates, teasers, discussions, follow me on IG. @datcrazywriter_ (Z)

Goodreads[1] :Z. S. STORM

---

1. https://www.goodreads.com/author/show/20744385.Zee_Shine_Storm

Don't miss out!

Visit the website below and you can sign up to receive emails whenever Z. S. STORM publishes a new book. There's no charge and no obligation.

https://books2read.com/r/B-A-TGXR-AKUMB

BOOKS2READ

Connecting independent readers to independent writers.